GREAT LIFE, GREAT FRIENDS, WHAT COULD GO WRONG?

Barbie ducked as streams of water shot back and forth between Lara and Nichelle. Soon Lara and Nichelle were chasing each other around the room. Both girls were careful to avoid Lara's work-in-progress, which stood propped on an easel near the front windows. Finally Lara and Nichelle collapsed on the tall stools by the counter, wheezing with laughter.

"So, Lara, do you know what you're going to do for the competition?" Nichelle repeated once she'd caught her breath.

"*Oui!*" Lara said excitedly. "I am doing a New York theme that combines painting and photos!"

Lara blotted water from her sleeve with a dry paper towel. Then she grabbed a trash can and started mopping up the mess she and Nichelle had made. "That is da bomb!" Nichelle said. "But won't it be hard to do?"

Nichelle slipped off her stool and helped Lara pick up the mounds of wet paper towels.

"*Oui,* it will be difficult," replied Lara, waving a brush in the air. "But now that I am inspired, it will be easy — just like that." She snapped her fingers. "It is . . . in the sack?"

"In the bag," said Nichelle, laughing.

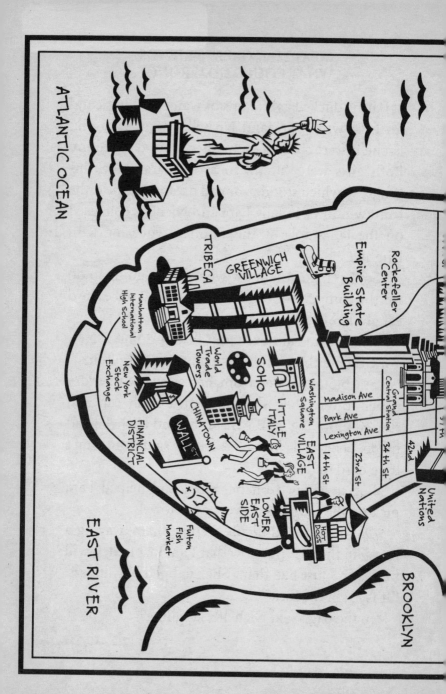

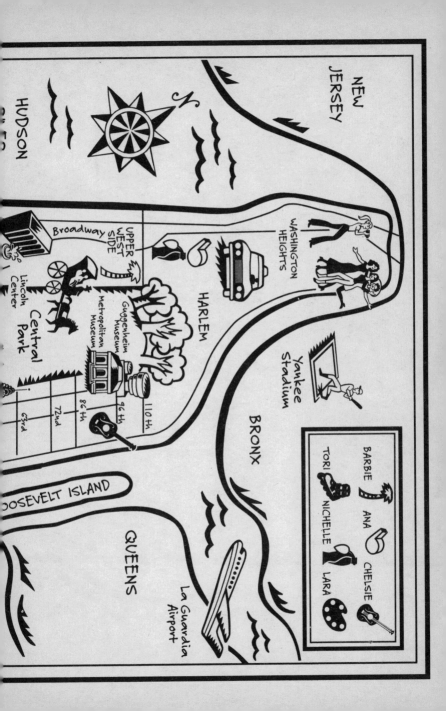

#5

Picture

Perfect?

By Melanie Stewart

A GOLD KEY PAPERBACK
Golden Books Publishing Company, Inc.
New York

A GOLD KEY Paperback Original

Golden Books Publishing Company, Inc.
888 Seventh Avenue
New York, NY 10106

Cover photography by Graham Kuhn

Interior art by Amy Bryant

ISBN: 0-307-23454-1

First Gold Key paperback printing August 1999

10 9 8 7 6 5 4 3 2 1

Printed in the U.S.A.

GENERATI*N GIRL

Picture Perfect?

Chapter 1

"Eureka!"

"**E**ureka! I have it!" Lara Morelli-Strauss waved her paintbrush in the air, splattering dark blue paint all over the canvas in front of her.

"Argh!" she said, stamping her foot in aggravation. Quickly, she blended white paint into the blue splatter that had landed on the background of her painting of the Statue of Liberty. There, that was better.

Both she and her friend Barbie Roberts had been in the Manhattan International High art room for at least an hour, waiting for their friends. Usually, Lara would have been impatient, waiting this long.

But for once, Lara was glad her friends had so many after-school activities. It gave her more time to paint, and with the New Artists' Competition coming up, she needed every minute she could get.

Barbie looked up from her math textbook and smiled. "So you've finally figured out what you're going to do for the art contest?" she asked.

"Finally," Lara said with a sigh. "And I got a wonderful idea from you, Barbie."

"Really? What are you going to do?" Barbie asked.

"I'm going to include photos we've taken of New York!"

The New Artists' Competition entry deadline was less than a month away, and Lara had been thinking of nothing else all semester. It wasn't an easy project to plan: It had to be a mixed-media work, using more than one kind of art. And Lara knew she had to come up with a really spectacular idea or she wouldn't even qualify. It had been one thing for her to win a school art prize at her old high school in Paris, but quite another to compete against some of the best young-adult artists in New York City for a $5,000 prize!

Barbie clapped her hands. "Painting combined with photography! That will be great!"

Picture Perfect?

Lara was born in France and had attended art school in Paris before moving to New York. But, surprisingly, she hadn't had much experience working with photography. An all-American girl from Malibu, California, Barbie had been a photography nut since she was a little kid. From the moment Lara and Barbie had met on the first day of school, the two had bonded. Since then, Barbie had been more than happy to teach Lara everything she knew about camera work.

Now Lara loved photography almost as much as Barbie did and, cameras in hand, the two friends would roam all over New York on their in-line skates, trying to capture the perfect shot. Their photo albums were full of pictures of pushcart vendors selling oysters in Little Italy, dancing dragons in Chinatown parades, and (Lara's favorite) little kids staring up openmouthed at the dinosaurs at the American Museum of Natural History. It was great!

Lara's stomach rumbled. "I wish they'd all hurry up," she said. "I'm starving!"

Barbie looked at her watch. "Ana's track practice will be over soon. Everyone has to be here by then."

It was almost dark outside. In the I. H. schoolroom window, the reflection of the two girls was a study in contrasts. Lara was tall and intense, and her long black hair was pinned up with a green jeweled clip that matched her eyes. Even after six months in New York, she still looked very European. Barbie was also tall, but an easygoing West Coast girl with long blond hair and blue eyes, wearing her favorite jeans and a denim jacket.

As Lara began to clean her brushes, a pretty African-American girl in a neon green dress stuck her head inside the door. "Anybody home?"

"Allo, Nichelle," Lara said.

"So, how's the art project going?" Nichelle Watson asked, slinging her silver backpack down on the table. "Whoops!" she said, jerking it back up again to avoid a puddle of oil paint. "Looks like the art project's going everywhere, girl." Then Nichelle moved a stack of blank canvases off a stool and sat down.

Lara smiled and said, "You know I'm not very neat when I paint, Mademoiselle Watson, so watch out!" She splashed Nichelle with tiny droplets of clean water from her newly washed brushes.

Nichelle made a face, pretending to be mad. Then she pulled her brand-new sports water bottle from her backpack. "Don't make me use this!"

Nichelle said, laughing. Lara held both hands up as if in surrender. Then, when Nichelle lowered her guard, she flicked more water at her friend.

"Okay, you asked for it," Nichelle said, squirting Lara right back.

"This is war!" Lara exclaimed.

Barbie ducked as streams of water shot back and forth between Lara and Nichelle. Soon Lara and Nichelle were chasing each other around the room, armed with wet paper towels. Both girls were careful to avoid Lara's work-in-progress, which stood propped on an easel near the front windows. Finally Lara and Nichelle collapsed back down on the tall stools by the counter, wheezing with laughter.

Lara regarded her friend with admiration. Nichelle was always bubbling with energy, rushing from one project to the next. Not only was she an A student and active in student government, but she was also working on a modeling career. How did she do it all?

"So, Lara, do you know what you're going to do for the competition?" Nichelle repeated once she'd caught her breath.

"*Oui!*" Lara said excitedly. "I am doing a New York theme that combines painting and photos!"

Lara blotted water from her sleeve with a dry paper towel. Then she grabbed a trash can and started mopping up the mess she and Nichelle had made. "That is da bomb!" Nichelle said. "But won't it be hard to do?"

Nichelle slipped off her stool and helped Lara pick up the mounds of wet paper towels.

"*Oui,* it will be difficult," replied Lara, waving a brush in the air. "But now that I am inspired, it will be easy — just like that." She snapped her fingers. "It is . . . in the sack?"

"In the bag," said Nichelle, laughing.

"In the bag, in the sack," Lara said with a sigh. "English is so crazy."

"Are you insulting the Queen's English?" a voice called out from behind them. Lara knew instantly who had entered the room. There was no mistaking that upper-class British accent. It was Chelsie Peterson.

"Hi, Chelsie," Lara said.

"Well," Nichelle said in a fake British accent, "you Brits may have invented our language, but we made it fun!"

Picture Perfect?

"And we perfected it, mate," interjected a girl with two long blond ponytails who had just skated into the room.

"About time you got here, Ms. Burns," Nichelle said jokingly.

Tori Burns laughed and skated in a slow circle around Nichelle. A tall, athletic exchange student from Melbourne, Australia, Tori was seriously into extreme sports. Her speech was always full of colorful Australian expressions nobody quite understood. "It took us Aussies to really perfect the language!" Tori smiled at Nichelle, then did a dazzling twirl. "Now can all you boofheads wrap things up here so we can get some grub? I'm dying for a cheeseburger."

"We're still waiting for Ana," Barbie said. "Then we'll hit Eatz!" Eatz was the girls' favorite hangout, a cool little diner about one block from the school. The food wasn't wonderful, but the prices were cheap and the owner didn't mind the place being mobbed by I. H. students after school.

"Oh, I'll be dead of hunger by the time Ana gets here," Tori said, groaning.

"Just wasting away waiting for me, is that it?" Ana said, jogging into the room in her green-and-gold

I. H. tracksuit. Lara grinned. Ana Suarez's family was originally from Mexico, but as far as Ana was concerned, New York was the center of the universe. Ana knew the city better than anyone. "So, let's go already."

Lara was so happy that she had such different friends. In Paris, her friends from the art school talked only about one thing: art. In New York, she had made new friends who were interested in a hundred different things, and they had helped make her life so much richer. She'd been to skateboarding competitions with Tori, helped Barbie rehearse for her acting auditions, cheered Ana across the finish line at the Central Park Triathlon, sung songs that Chelsie had written for the school musical, and helped Nichelle pick out outfits for her modeling portfolio. There was never a dull moment.

Lara finished cleaning her brushes quickly, and they all set off for Eatz.

At the diner, the girls squashed into one tiny booth, three on each side. So what if they could hardly move? It was either the booth or stand, and with the boisterous crowd of I. H. students, none of them wanted to risk it.

Picture Perfect?

Chelsie opened the entertainment section of the newspaper and pointed to an ad for *Angel Fire,* the latest Troy Marcus film. "Oh, isn't he gorgeous?" She sighed. "We have to go see it." The girls had arranged to see a movie tonight. But with all their different interests, how were they ever going to decide which movie to see? Tori liked action movies, Barbie liked love stories, Nichelle and Ana liked thrillers, and Chelsie — well, Chelsie liked any movie that had Troy Marcus in it. Lara liked European films herself, but she was willing to go with Chelsie's movie choice for tonight. Troy Marcus was extremely cute!

Nichelle took the lead in making a quick decision. "So, what do we think? All those in favor of *Angel Fire,* raise your hands."

Six hands went up. "Unbelievable," Tori said. "We all agree!"

"A new first in 'Generation Girl' history!" Barbie said. Barbie and her five best friends all worked on their school newspaper, the *Generation Beat.* They sometimes called themselves the Generation Girls.

Just then the waiter appeared. "What will it be today, girls?" he asked.

After they had all ordered, Nichelle turned to a

new subject. "Hey, have you guys sent in any nominations for the 'Principal-for-a-Day' event?"

The 'Principal-for-a-Day' event was the brainchild of Principal Simmons, who was trying to generate publicity for the brand-new International High. She was aiming for celebrities, movie stars, or politicians. But she wanted the winner to be someone the students wanted, as well. So the *I. H. Generation Beat*, the student newspaper and website, started a poll to collect nominations.

Chelsie cleared her throat loudly. "If any of you haven't yet sent in your nominations," she said, "I suggest you do so soon." As Assistant Managing Editor of the *I. H. Generation Beat*, Chelsie had been put in charge of counting all the ballots.

"Watch your backs," hollered their waiter. "Hot food, coming up." They all made room on the table, but he still had trouble finding room for all the plates.

Nichelle dumped all the baskets of french fries onto one big plate in the middle. "We'll all just share," she said. Everybody stopped talking to focus on eating.

Just as Lara took the very last bite of her burger,

Picture Perfect?

Just as Lara took the very last bite of her burger, Barbie looked at her watch and squeaked in dismay. "We have to run! We're going to miss the movie." She quickly figured out the bill on her calculator. Then the girls snatched up their backpacks and decamped from the booth in a rush up to the cash register. Lara ran back to the table to leave a tip for the waiter after they paid the bill.

"No time to wait for all you pedestrians," Ana said outside of Eatz, pocketing her change. "We'll buy the tickets for everybody, and you can pay us back." She and Tori threw on their in-line skates and skated ahead to the theater. Barbie, Lara, Chelsie, and Nichelle ran in their wake.

Chelsie was panting after a couple of blocks. As they dashed across the street, narrowly dodging a speeding taxi, she wheezed, "Oh, I'm going to faint right here on the sidewalk." She slowed to a walk for a minute. "I am so out of shape."

They caught up to Ana and Tori at the theater. "About time, slowpokes," Tori said, fanning the six tickets out in her hand. "Fortunately, we managed to get the last tickets."

Lara stopped in front of the NOW PLAYING movie poster for *Angel Fire*. In the poster, Troy Marcus was leading a gorgeous actress down a twisty street with a weapon in one hand.

As the girls filed into the packed theater, Lara smacked her forehead in annoyance. "Save me a seat, Chelsie," Lara whispered.

"Are you getting popcorn?" Chelsie whispered back.

"No, I forgot to tell my parents we were going to a movie tonight. I have to call them."

Lara dashed out into the hallway, searching for a pay phone. She hated missing the trailers! Finally, she found the phone by the water fountains.

She dialed. Her mother's voice answered, sounding upset. "*Pronto!* I mean, *buongiorno!*" she said. Mama was Italian and she could never remember to answer the phone in English.

"*Ciao,* Mama," Lara said. "Hi."

"Oh, hello, *carina!*" she said when she heard Lara's voice. Lara's mother couldn't resist calling her daughter her pet name — "pretty one" — in Italian.

Lara heard pots banging around in the background. "I'm making some lasagna in the kitchen," her mother said. "Are you coming home soon?"

A male voice in the kitchen interrupted Lara's

mom. "Lucia, must you make so much noise? I am trying to work!" Lara knew this voice almost as well as her own. It was her father's.

"I am talking to Lara!" her mother shouted back at him. "And I am making dinner. Is that permitted?"

Lara winced. Mama and Papa always seemed to be arguing about something. Lara was used to it, but she didn't like it. Not for the first time, Lara wished her Italian mother and German father were a little more compatible. Mama's nature was as emotional and excitable as Papa's was quiet and restrained.

Lara sighed, waiting for them to stop arguing.

"I am sorry, *carina*, what were we talking about?" her mother said.

"Dinner," Lara replied. "It is a no tonight. I am going to a movie with my friends. But I'll be home by about nine-thirty. I'll eat some supper then."

"All right, my darling, have a good time," said her mother.

Just then Papa picked up the extension in his study. "Lara, *liebchen* — darling — I haff a question for you," he said in a heavy German accent. "Haff you seen my German-English dictionary?

Your mother keeps moving it around to make room for her fashion design sketches."

Lara sighed again. "No, Papa, I haven't seen it." She told both her parents that the movie was about to start, and they said good-bye.

Walking back into the darkened theater, Lara thought about her parents and their conflicts. They'd moved to New York because Papa had been offered a visiting professorship in German literature at New York University. Mama was a successful fashion designer in Europe and had thrown herself right into New York's fashion scene as soon as they'd arrived. Mama loved New York. And Lara was thrilled to get the chance to attend International High. But Papa was a different story. Lara didn't think he was really happy in this loud, brash city, even though he loved teaching.

More than anything else, Papa liked to sit and read quietly. But with Mama always in motion, and all of Lara's friends from I. H. using the loft as a base for their SoHo excursions, peace and quiet were always in short supply. It was especially difficult because of the way their apartment was laid out. The loft was basically one big open space, with a few rooms carved out of it for a bit of privacy. But every sound bounced all over the loft, shattering his concentration.

Mama, on the other hand, thrived on commotion. She always wanted to be out, going to art galleries and fancy boutiques with her fashion designer friends. With new patterns and fabrics scattered everywhere, Mama's fashion design studio at the far end of the loft was as chaotic as Papa's office was neat and organized. It drove her crazy when Papa buried himself for weeks at a time in his books.

Lara felt one of her headaches coming on. Back in Europe, her parents' little arguments had just been part of life. But these days it seemed different, and Lara didn't know why. She forced herself to stop thinking about it as she squeezed down the row past Barbie and Tori and took her seat between Chelsie and Nichelle. The trailers were just ending. "Good timing!" Nichelle whispered.

The movie was surprisingly good. Despite herself, Lara had to admit Troy was very, very handsome.

"Can you believe she trusts him?" Nichelle whispered to Lara as the heroine climbed into the bad guy's car. "He is so clearly a terrorist."

Glass shattered as Troy Marcus dove through a window, rescuing the leading lady from an international terrorist group. Then he pulled a bouquet of roses from the back of his motorcycle and presented it to her as they drove away with the bad guys in hot pursuit.

But later, as Lara watched the movie, her mind couldn't help drifting back to her parents. Had they ever been that romantic? She knew that Americans had an expression, "opposites attract." But in the case of her parents, the expression just didn't seem to apply anymore, if it ever had. A car exploded on the movie screen, startling her. She'd lost the whole thread of the movie, worrying about her parents. What's worse, her headache had not left her.

Chelsie grabbed her arm. "Isn't Troy the greatest?"

Lara nodded and whispered back, "*Absolutement!*"

Nichelle pulled some chocolate truffles out of her backpack and she passed one down to Lara. She munched chocolate and watched Troy Marcus. Life was much better with chocolate in it. As Lara relaxed again and enjoyed the movie, her headache

Picture Perfect?

faded away. *I should stop worrying so much,* Lara thought.

After the movie (and long after the chocolate had run out), the girls filtered out onto the street. Nichelle and Tori started to sing a tune Chelsie had written for the sophomore class school musical as they walked along toward the subway station. Soon, Chelsie, Lara, Barbie, and Ana all joined in, singing at the tops of their lungs in three-part harmony.

Nichelle broke off singing. "Hey, Lara," she said. "Isn't that one of your mother's designs?" She pointed at an outfit in the window of a trendy boutique. The dress looked a little bit Japanese but was done in purple linen rather than in silk, and was trimmed with velvet.

"*Oui!*" said Lara, marveling at Nichelle's eye for detail. Mama had a gift for anticipating trends and creating strikingly unusual looks. As Mama's unofficial tester, Lara had a whole closet full of cutting-edge clothes that she let her friends borrow whenever they liked.

"Your parents are so cool, Lara," Nichelle said. "You don't have to follow a million rules like I do. You can really be creative."

Chelsie sighed, "And you live in SoHo, with all those art galleries. Your life is just perfect."

"Simply *parfait*," Barbie said, practicing her French.

Parfait meant "perfect" in French. But despite what her friends thought, Lara didn't think life with her parents was perfect in any language.

"Can we talk about something else?" Lara said.

"Too right!" said Tori, executing a beautiful little pirouette on the street corner. "The only parfait I care about is one full of ice cream!"

"Okay, let's go to New York Freeze," Ana said. New York Freeze always had a long line of people waiting outside, and the owner was famously rude to everyone. But the ice cream was the best in the city, and the girls never missed a chance to go there.

"Do you think Troy Marcus knows French?" Chelsie asked as they walked on. "Then I could write him in the language of love. Oh, Troy, *mon amour!*" she exclaimed in a theatrical tone of voice. She had already sent away twice for Troy's photo but hadn't heard back yet.

"Give it up, girl," Nichelle said to Chelsie. "He's just another Hollywood face."

Picture Perfect?

Chelsie shook her head. "He works for the homeless and for Greenpeace. He's my ideal man — gorgeous and caring."

Tori gagged herself with a finger. "Ooooh, I'm going to recycle my lunch! He's so gorgeous," Tori imitated. "So caring and wonderful and amazing." Tori lay down on the bus bench and roared with laughter. Now Ana and Chelsie were giggling, too.

"Well, I submitted Troy's name for 'Principal-for-a-Day,' I'll have you know!" Chelsie said. "I bet he wins the nomination in a breeze."

Chapter 2

Van Gogh and
Tater Tots

Lara had advanced algebra for her first class in the morning, which was lucky. She had always found math to be her easiest subject. Numbers were the same in any language.

Since she was ahead of the class, she zoned out during the lecture to think about her art project. Lara knew she wanted to use her photographs and her painting together somehow, but she hadn't worked out all the details yet.

She'd been painting the Statue of Liberty on a mural-sized canvas, with dark storm clouds drifting over the lights of the ships in the harbor. She had smeared a layer of plaster on the canvas to give it a little texture before she'd started painting, and the effect was really working. Yesterday, she'd painted in a blurry figure of a young girl standing on the deck of the ferry, trying to see the Statue of Liberty through the fog.

Lara had been inspired to add the figure of the girl to the picture after her weekly volunteer session at Rainbow House, one of the few homeless shelters in New York with space for homeless families.

She'd gotten involved with Rainbow House while working on an assignment for the *I. H. Generation Beat*. The article she and Chelsie had written about homelessness and the Rainbow House shelter had led I. H. to adopt the shelter as a school charity. Lots of students volunteered there now, and the canned food drive that she and Barbie had chaired had collected so much food that they had enough left over to send to other shelters across the city.

She'd first seen the girl about a month ago, early in her volunteer shift at Rainbow House. It had been raining all day, and the converted YMCA building where the shelter was located smelled damp and musty like an old gym locker. One of the things she liked about Rainbow House was that Mrs. Johnson, the director, didn't care that Lara was only fifteen. Mrs. Johnson, a short, plump, gray-haired whirlwind, didn't care much about rules at all. She just cared about getting things done. She knew Lara was as competent as any grown-up. She assigned Lara to do whatever needed to be done, from making up beds, to sorting donations, to chopping vegetables for dinner in the kitchen.

Lara had been folding baby clothes from the new donations when she saw a thin, careworn-looking woman come in out of the pouring rain, with four kids. The oldest daughter, who couldn't have been more than eleven, had been carrying her two-year-old brother on her hip, and they were both soaked. Lara started passing out blankets and toys to the kids. She was struck by the look on the girl's face as she bent to comfort her little brother, wrapping him in both blankets and leaving none for herself. Her two younger sisters snatched the dolls from Lara's hands and dashed off happily to play with them in the kids' area. But the older girl shook her head, wringing out her wet hair, and said, "No toy for me, thanks."

Picture Perfect?

Lara wanted to say something to her, but she couldn't think of what. She settled for, "It is cold outside, no? Come and sit down by the heater."

The girl thanked her and settled the boy, still wrapped up in two blankets, down at her feet. Then she sat down behind him, and he leaned back on her. She took care of the little boy so tenderly, it reminded Lara of paintings she'd seen in the Vatican when they lived in Rome. The girl's mother sat down wearily beside her with a *thump* and put her arm around her daughter and her son, hugging them both at the same time. "Everything's going to be all right, you'll see," the woman told them. "We'll be warm and dry in no time at all."

Lara made up beds for the family as far from the door as possible so they could have a little privacy and be out of the cold. She wanted to make things as nice as she could for them. Later that night when she was home in SoHo, she'd lain awake in bed until after midnight, just staring out the window. It was only after she'd pulled out a drawing pad and sketched the girl that she was finally able to go to sleep.

Lara had gone back to the shelter the next day after school, even though it wasn't her regular day, to see if she could find the family again. She wanted to do more for them, even if she didn't know what. But they were gone, checked out early that morning, and no one knew where they had gone.

The bell rang, signaling the end of class and jarring Lara out of her memories. Working at the homeless shelter was one of the best things she had done since she had come to New York. It was sad, but she knew she was doing something important. She waved at Chelsie as they passed in the hall. But there was no time to talk; she was off to Mr. Ordway's Latin class.

Why, oh, why had she let Papa talk her into taking Latin as her language for this year? He'd explained that it would help her with grammar and vocabulary in Italian, French, and English, and of course he was right. But she was so tired of hearing about Caesar and his travels, she could just die. Wasn't there anything else written in Latin?

Thank goodness she had lunch with Tori third period. She could probably hold off dying of boredom until then. It was crazy having such an early lunch, though. She felt as if she had barely even finished breakfast. All her other friends didn't have lunch for another hour.

The cafeteria was only half full when Lara got there, with the other early lunch orphans milling around checking out the special of the day. Lara joined Tori in the serving line.

"Mystery meat in glue sauce again," Tori said. "What a shocker." They inspected the choices glumly as they approached the head of the line.

"I think I will have the caviar, then the delicious Fettuccine Alfredo, and the Baked Alaska for dessert," Lara said in the most upper-class voice she could manage.

Tori said, "And I'll have the prime rib and baked potato followed by the double-chocolate mousse."

"Pizza, Tater Tots, and creamed spinach, coming right up," said Mrs. Morgenthau, wiping pizza sauce onto her white apron. She dropped plates of food onto the girls' trays and adjusted her hair net. "We're fresh out of caviar," she added. Lara and Tori looked at each other and giggled.

The two girls found an empty table and plopped down their trays. Tori prodded at her pizza with a fork. Lara was already eating hers, blowing frantically on it to avoid the dreaded pizza-cheese mouth burn. "Hurry up, Tori," she said. "I have to run upstairs to the newspaper office!" Lara was Art Director of the *I. H. Generation Beat*. She wanted to look at her portfolio of photos from the homeless shelter story to see if they would give her any more ideas for her art project.

"Okay, hold your horses," Tori said, swallowing her last bite of pizza. "I'll go up there with you." Tori designed the *I. H. Generation Beat* web page.

Up at the newspaper office on the seventh floor, Lara studied her black-and-white photos of Rainbow House, and the glimmer of an idea struck her just as the class bell rang. She and Tori frantically raced down the seven flights of stairs to Mr. Budge's history class. The escalators and elevators were still not working, which wasn't surprising since the engineers who were supposed to install them had disappeared without a trace on a lunch break and never returned. What artist had to put up with this? Lara wondered. Did van Gogh have to create between class bells?

Next period was art appreciation, with the dreamy Mr. Harris. When Lara came into the classroom, he was already setting up the slide projector.

Picture Perfect?

Lara slid into her regular desk in the front row next to Chelsie.

Chelsie was so excited, she was practically jumping up and down in her seat. "Guess what?" she bubbled. "We counted up the poll votes, and Troy won! Overwhelmingly! And guess what? Mrs. Simmons gave me permission to write to him!"

"How did you do that?" asked Lara.

"I begged," said Chelsie. "Shamelessly." Lara smiled.

"I'm supposed to ask him to be 'Principal-for-a-Day,'" Chelsie went on. "And I read in *People* magazine that he's going to be in New York for a whole week for a movie promotion, so he might — he just might — say yes. Just think of it, Troy Marcus in the halls of our very own school!" She clasped an envelope to her chest. "I can't wait for school to be over so I can mail this!"

Mr. Harris started the slide projector. The first slide was of a beautiful French cathedral — upside down. *Just one of those days,* Lara thought. The pizza rumbled on one side of her stomach. The Tater Tots rumbled back from the other.

Next, van Gogh's *Self-Portrait* popped up on the slide sideways. *I bet van Gogh would have loved*

Tater Tots, Lara thought. She propped open her sketch pad as Mr. Harris lectured. Quickly, she copied van Gogh's portrait, but added a Tater Tot sticking out of his mouth. She added a cafeteria table and chair, and penciled in her title underneath the sketch: *van Gogh with Tater Tot.* There: She'd introduced van Gogh to a whole new exciting cuisine. Too bad he couldn't thank her!

Chapter 3

"And the Winner Is . . ."

Two weeks later, Lara was feeling on top of the world. Her art project was going so well. She'd finally decided exactly how she was going to do the piece for the New Artists' Competition. It would mean she would have to do three paintings, but she could do it. The first and biggest one, her painting of the Statue of Liberty in the harbor, was already almost done. Only the figure of the girl on the ferry remained unfinished.

Lara had planned her exhibit carefully. The Statue of Liberty would be the first painting the judges would see, hanging on the wall directly in front of them. Then Lara would hang the other two paintings by wires from the ceiling on each side of the big painting. These two paintings were both of Rainbow House, one showing the outside of the shelter, and one showing the inside.

It was in the paintings of Rainbow House that Lara was going to use her photos. She was proud of her idea. Lara planned to attach photographs of people and places right to the canvas, and paint around them to make them part of the picture. It wouldn't be easy to get it right. Lara had never done anything like it before. But she was up for the challenge.

She'd taken a lot of photos documenting every bit of the inside of Rainbow House so she could get the proportions right when she painted it. And she'd taken pictures of the staff and the people who stayed there. She'd asked permission first, and not everybody had said yes. Some of the residents of the shelter had taken offense. They'd said that she was only interested in photographing them because she had a project to do, not because she was really interested in their lives. One man had put it harshly: "I don't want to be homeless forever in some kid's stupid painting."

Lara had started to wonder if she was really

doing the right thing. Was she just using Rainbow House as an art project? She didn't want people to think she was just using them. That wasn't why she was at Rainbow House.

It was Barbie who had urged her to continue. As they were washing dishes at the end of their volunteer shift one day, Barbie had said, "Those judges and all the people who will see the exhibition don't have any idea how much good a place like Rainbow House really does for homeless families. If you can open their eyes for them, then it's worth doing."

So Lara had gone back to work on it. It was amazing how well the photos of people's faces meshed with the painting.

Lunch period was practically over, and Lara's hands were getting tired. She rinsed off her brushes and put them away just as Chelsie burst into the room.

"You'll never guess what's happened!" Chelsie shrieked. "It's so fantastically amazing!"

"What?"

"No, guess." Chelsie was ecstatic. "Go on, guess."

Lara thought back to the last time she'd seen Chelsie this happy. "Troy Marcus is coming?"

"Yes!" Chelsie screamed.

"No!" Lara said, totally amazed. "Not really?"

"It's true, it's true, it's true," Chelsie sang as she grabbed Lara's hands and danced her around the room. "Mr. Merlin is going to make the announcement right after lunch is over, but I just had to tell you first. Oh, I'm going to run and tell Barbie right this second."

"Chelsie, wait, what do you think of my painting?" Lara asked. But it was too late. Chelsie was already gone.

By the time the PA speaker crackled on at the beginning of fifth period, the word had spread like wildfire. There was a thrilled murmur of voices, and then silence as Mr. Merlin's voice, crackling with static, came over the system.

"Attention, students . . . attention, students." Mr. Merlin never said anything once when he could do so twice. "We have a tidbit of interesting news."

"Is he coming or isn't he?" said a girl at the front of the room.

Mr. Merlin cleared his throat, "As you may have guessed, my special announcement has to do with the 'Principal-for-a-Day' nominations."

"Oh, boy, will he ever get to the point?" a boy said from the third row.

Picture Perfect?

The PA system cut off briefly, then came back on long enough for the students to hear Principal Simmons say, "Oliver, is that thing on?"

Everybody around Lara laughed. The PA system was famous for fading in and out at the wrong times, and for cutting off the actual announcements.

"We have a winner, and our winner has accepted the position," Mr. Merlin said, and his usually dry, quiet voice sounded almost excited.

A hush fell over the classrooms, the auditorium, even basketball practice in the gym.

Mr. Merlin continued: "Our 'Principal-for-a-Day' will be the Hollywood film star Troy Marcus!"

The school exploded in cheers. You could hear the noise from the first to the seventh floor. The instant the bell rang, everyone burst out into the hall in an unofficial recess. Lara, Barbie, and their friends all met down the hall from Mr. Harris's classroom to congratulate Chelsie.

"You really did it," Lara said, giving Chelsie a giant hug.

Nichelle and Ana exchanged high fives. "Chelsie, you rule this school as far as I'm concerned," Nichelle said.

Ana agreed, "That goes double for me. Man, the TV stations are going to be all over this!"

Barbie was about to congratulate Chelsie, when Principal Simmons and Assistant Principal Merlin suddenly appeared. Principal Simmons was holding something out to Chelsie. "I have something for you, Chelsie," she said, smiling. "These were delivered to the office."

Chelsie's mouth hung open with shock. "Roses!" she cried. "They're beautiful!"

Lara said, "Chelsie, there's a card. What does it say?"

Chelsie opened the tiny envelope. Inside was a typed card that said:

To the nicest fan a star could have. Love, Troy.

All the girls screamed. "He wrote back," Chelsie said. "I knew he would! Oh, I am saving this card forever and ever. He sent me roses."

Chelsie carried the roses the rest of the day, carefully ensconced in Lara's extra paintbrush holder full of water. Chelsie was the undisputed hero of the school.

At the end of classes, Lara was amazed to hear a

loud rumble in the hallway. "What on earth is this noise?" she asked Barbie.

"I don't believe it," Barbie answered. "I think they're actually fixing the escalator!"

They saw Assistant Principal Merlin talking to a whole group of repairmen, led by Poogy the janitor. "Everything in this building must be in working order two weeks from today," he was telling them. "Everything. The escalators, the elevators, the water fountains, the squeaky doors, the leaky plumbing. Troy Marcus is coming to visit!"

Lara noticed that Assistant Principal Merlin had forgotten to mention the defective PA system. Oh, well. Troy Marcus was going to be principal, her art project was going to be done on time, and the escalators were going to be fixed. There'd been enough miracles for one day.

Chapter 4

What's Going On?

Lara still missed Paris dreadfully, but she had to admit New York was pretty exciting. SoHo was the heart of New York's contemporary art community. More than half their neighbors in the building were artists. And there were five or six art galleries on every block, which, for Lara, was like having her choice of dozens of candy stores. Every kind of art in the world was right there!

Papa had built a separate space in the loft for Lara's studio, which was where she was painting now. It had a raised platform made out of plywood. But the only way to get up to the platform

Picture Perfect?

was by climbing a rickety wooden ladder. And she was always forgetting and leaving things, which meant a million trips up and down the ladder. Her own personal ladder workout. Up and down, up and down — who needed a gym?

The studio was still pretty great, though, for all she complained about the ladder. The raised platform, with lots of sunlight from the giant windows, was the perfect place to paint. She liked it enough to lug an inflatable air mattress up the ladder so she could sleep up there. Her oil paints and easel stood at one end of the platform, the air mattress on the other end, and her black-and-white photos hung from clotheslines that crisscrossed the rest of it.

Lara chewed the end of her brush. Now where had she left her new tubes of oil paint? She knew she had brought them home from school. They had to be here somewhere. She searched her whole studio platform, and then threw her smock down on the plywood floor in aggravation. She remembered that she'd left her new oil paints in her backpack at the base of the ladder, and she had to climb back down to get them.

Lara paused as she climbed down the ladder. She

could hear her parents' arguing voices echoing from somewhere else in the loft. She couldn't see them. But the way the sound carried, they could have been right next to her. She grabbed her backpack quickly and climbed back up to her loft space immediately.

Suddenly, Lara felt too miserable to paint. She sat down at the edge of the platform with her legs hanging over the side. It was as if her parents thought she was invisible. Didn't they realize that their voices carried? She didn't want to listen, but she couldn't quite stop herself.

It wasn't a new argument at all, but Mama really did sound extra aggravated. She was arguing in Italian, not English. "Friedrich, you drive me crazy! You sit in your study, revising and revising! I miss you. Lara misses you."

It was true, Papa had been pretty much missing in action over the past month. He was publishing a big article for some German magazine. Lara always dreaded his articles because he was such a perfectionist. Every word had to be exactly right, no matter how long it took, and the loft had to be completely quiet while he worked.

The night before last, Lara had been sleeping in her loft when she heard a noise downstairs after midnight. She had snuck down the studio ladder with her miniature flashlight held in her teeth. It was Papa, sitting at the big wooden table in his pajamas with his glasses sliding down his nose, flipping through the pages of a book.

"Oh, Papa, it's just you," she had said in a whisper. "I thought it might be a burglar."

"No, *liebchen*," Papa had chuckled. "Just your old father looking for some peace and quiet. Except, of course, I dropped a book and voke you up. I'm sorry, Lara. Go off to bed. You need all your sleep."

"So do you, Papa," she'd lectured him. "How will you teach your classes tomorrow?"

"In my sleep," he'd whispered back, smiling. "I vork at my book all night like this so I can sleep during my lectures like my students." This was just silly talk, Lara knew. Papa's students all loved him.

Lara had rolled her eyes at him. Then she'd made them each a cup of hot chocolate and gone back to bed. As boring as all that quiet and order seemed to Lara, she knew he loved it, so it was okay with her.

But listening to her parents argue now, she noticed how tired Papa sounded. Had he been staying up late all week? Maybe she shouldn't have her friends over for a while.

"I haff a deadline, Lucia," Papa said in a tired voice. "Everything has to be right. I vill be embarrassed if the footnotes are wrong." His English still had a heavy German accent.

Lara didn't think Mama had ever made a deadline on time in her life, or cared about it, either. Sure enough, Mama said, "So, a deadline is more important than we are?"

Mama was so different from Papa, it amazed Lara they'd ever fallen in love. It was actually art that had brought them together. Papa had been a brand-new assistant professor, and Mama had been a graduate student at the Sorbonne University in Paris. On a field trip to the Louvre museum, Papa had dropped his textbook on Mama's foot right in front of the *Mona Lisa*. Three months later, they were married.

Three months! It seemed sort of quick to get married. But they'd been, as Mama put it, "madly in love." Lara guessed that it must have been love that had blinded them to the fact that they didn't have a thing in common.

Downstairs, Mama yelled, "Oh, you and your books!" Lara could imagine her throwing her hands in the air, pacing around the kitchen. "Oh, *scusi!* Excuse me! I'm sorry that your family interferes with your books. I think sometimes you love them more than you love us!"

"Lucia, darling, you know that is not true." Papa's voice sounded as calm as ever. It didn't mean he wasn't listening, Lara knew. Papa would sound just like that if the house was burning down. But she knew it would make Mama even more annoyed. "Hand me that book on the counter, vill you?"

Lara put her head in her hands. Papa could be so clueless sometimes, it just amazed her! He couldn't have picked a better way to bug Mama if he'd tried on purpose.

"Honestly, Friedrich, you haven't really heard a word I've said!" Mama was really worked up now. "I came home early so we could all have dinner together. But if you're too busy, then forget it! I will take Lara and we will go out to dinner. Go back to your books!" Mama's tone softened a little. "Should we bring you something back to eat? I know how you forget to eat when you write."

"No, I vill heat up some leftover strudel. Don't worry, Lucia, I promise I'll eat."

"Hmmph!" Mama said.

Lara breathed a sigh of relief. It sounded like the argument was over. At least for now, anyway. And she'd be happy to take a dinner break, anyway. Her stomach rumbled at the thought. If she were getting somewhere with her art project, then she wouldn't have cared about food for a minute. Maybe she was a little like Papa after all.

Outside the loft, Lara and her mother caught a cab to the Stage Deli. Lara pushed open the heavy glass door of the restaurant, and the hostess sent them to an empty table at the back. The deli was buzzing with conversation around them as they each tore into a giant overstuffed corned beef sandwich with an extra pickle. Too bad Papa couldn't be there, too. He loved corned beef. By unspoken agreement, they ordered an extra sandwich for him, anyway, even though he'd told them not to bother.

"Listen, Lara . . ." Mama sounded unexpectedly serious, and she spoke in Italian instead of English. "I know I've been gone a lot lately, *carina.*"

It was true, her mother really had been gone more than usual. Between that and Papa's article, Lara had pretty much been on her own the past few weeks.

Picture Perfect?

"I figured you've been busy with your next show," Lara answered her in Italian. "And I've been busy, too, Mama, so don't worry." She patted her Mama's hand. "I do okay on my own."

For a second, Lara thought she must be seeing things. It looked as if Mama was going to cry.

Mama squeezed Lara's hand. "*Come sei bella,* Lara. You look beautiful. And you are so grown up." Mama blew her nose and continued. "But you are never on your own, Lara. No matter what, Papa and I are always right behind you. Always."

"Sure, Mama. I know that." Lara was mystified. Of course they were! They were her parents, weren't they? "Go work on your show." Lara made shooing motions. "Everything's fine."

Mama looked relieved. "I'll be home before nine o'clock, if you need help with your homework."

Help with my homework? Now Lara was really wondering what was up. She hadn't needed help with her homework since she was a kid. Mama knew that.

"No, that's okay, Mama. I'm going to a movie with Barbie, Chelsie, and Ana." Chelsie had wanted to see *Angel Fire* again, in honor of Troy's visit. "Remember, I asked you about it yesterday."

"Yes, I remember," Mama said, though she clearly hadn't. "Have a good time, then." Suddenly she reached over and gave Lara a huge, bone-cracking hug. "I love you so much, Lara!"

"I love you, too, Mama. I'll drop Papa's sandwich off at home before I leave."

Back home, she took the sandwich out of the paper bag and arranged it on a plate. Papa liked things to be orderly. He missed Munich a lot, Lara thought. New York wasn't an orderly place at all. She made him tea and carried the whole thing on a tray into his study.

Papa wasn't even studying. He was just sitting in his desk chair staring into space. Lara checked for evidence of strudel. None!

"Honestly, Papa, you really have to eat," Lara said.

Papa jumped. "Lara, *liebchen,* you startled me."

"Sorry, Papa." Lara held out the tray of food, but he didn't take it. "I brought you dinner. Just a corned beef sandwich and some tea. And a dill pickle, too. I know you must be hungry by now."

Papa shook himself a little and took the tray. "You are such a goot girl. Is your mother here?"

"No, she went straight back to the museum from

44

the restaurant." Lara wanted to ask if everything was okay, but she had a strong feeling that she shouldn't. "Is your article almost done?"

"No, I just sit und stare at this idiot computer, as you see." Papa pointed at the blank screen with one hand and tugged angrily at his hair with the other. "It goes nowhere!" He threw a book on the floor in frustration.

"Like my art project. I'm just wasting canvas today, I think." Lara faked a laugh. Papa was never like this. "Some days are just like that, Papa."

"Yes, you're probably right. Ve both need, how do you say, a break?" Papa smiled at Lara. "Vhat are you doing tonight? Do you vant to go get an ice cream vith your ancient father?"

"*Ja*, Papa!" Lara said in German, earning a real laugh from Papa. That was more like it. Papa had just been working too hard, that was all. Then Lara heard their doorbell buzz in the kitchen. She looked at her watch. "Oh, that must be Barbie and everybody."

Papa looked confused.

"We're all going to a movie tonight. But we can go for ice cream first, if you don't mind a lot of girls along. It will be fun!"

Papa laughed, "My little social butterfly. At least one of us has adjusted to New York. No, I don't vant to fight my way through a hundred teenage girls. I vill eat my sandwich in peace, and finish this article for goot."

He sounded better, anyway. "We'll go for ice cream tomorrow, okay, Papa?" Lara asked from the doorway of the study. The bell buzzed again.

Papa laughed and waved at Lara to go. "Have fun, *liebchen*. Say hi to the crazy American girls from me." Papa never remembered her friends' names. "Be home by ten o'clock."

"Ten? But Mama said I could stay out until eleven!"

Papa thought for a moment. "Ten-thirty. And ask me first next time. Your mother is too lenient."

"Okay, Papa. Bye!" Lara ran down the stairs to meet Barbie. She felt a little unsettled. Maybe it was just the corned beef. Was Papa really happy here? And why was Mama acting weird? Were everyone's parents like this?

Chapter 5

Thank Goodness for Chocolate!

L ara slammed her backpack down onto her desk so hard that the whole thing tipped forward, dumping her notebook and pencil case. This whole day had been impossible, and she wasn't even through first period yet. Mama and Papa had been arguing in the kitchen when Lara woke up. They'd switched into whispers as soon as they heard her alarm go off, which made it worse somehow. When she went into the kitchen for breakfast, they were talking in fake loud, cheerful voices. They'd been acting like this for weeks now. What kind of fight was it that they thought they had to hide it from her?

Then she'd missed her train and gotten to school so late, she'd had to get a hall pass from Assistant Principal Merlin. By the time he'd finished telling her a story about his old school and finally written out her pass, she'd missed half of advanced algebra.

Dr. Spool looked inquiringly over her bifocals at the noise of the chair legs banging against the floor. "Thank you for joining us today, Lara," she said dryly.

And to think she had just told Chelsie that advanced algebra was her favorite class! Usually, she really liked Dr. Spool, who told bad math jokes and took the class on field trips to learn about astronomy. But, today, Lara just couldn't seem to focus.

Ten minutes later, Dr. Spool called on Lara to solve a problem up at the chalkboard. On a regular day, this would have been a breeze. But Lara stared blankly at it for so long that Dr. Spool came and looked over her shoulder.

"Is everything okay, Lara?" he asked in a low tone.

Lara shook herself. She had never let her parents' arguing get to her before, and she wasn't about to start now. She scribbled the right answer on the blackboard without bothering to show the intermediate steps.

"I'm fine, Dr. Spool. I've just got a headache, that's all."

It wasn't actually a lie. She could feel the tiniest beginnings of a headache.

Back at her desk, Lara opened her textbook and began working through the homework problems she hadn't finished last night. Numbers didn't try to hide things from her, or change when she wasn't looking.

Lara walked into the hallway when class ended, still in a daze. Instead of the regular announcements, the hall bulletin boards were plastered with Troy Marcus movie posters. Lara tried to feel excited about his being "Principal-for-a-Day," the way she had been when she'd first found out, but she was so grouchy today, it just didn't work.

Mr. Ordway's Latin class only worsened her mood. She wished she had class with some of her friends. She needed someone to distract her from her worries. Well, chocolate would have to do, at least until she had lunch with Tori next period. Chocolate was big-time comfort food for Lara, and Grandmama had just sent her another "care package" crammed full of goodies all the way from Munich.

Lara snuck a chocolate bar out of her backpack the second Mr. Ordway turned his back to write the assignment on the board. She unwrapped the foil stealthily under her desk and then took a giant, delicious bite. Ordinarily she would have held out until lunch, but today she really needed it. Of course her mouth was still crammed full of chocolate when Mr. Ordway called on her to translate the next passage. It was just that kind of day.

When the bell rang at last, Lara leaped up to go meet Tori. Finally, a friend to talk to!

She didn't have to go far. Tori was getting lectured by Assistant Principal Merlin just outside Mr. Ordway's door. It was pretty clear why, too. Mr. Merlin was holding a skateboard in his hand, and it didn't take the giant blue AUSSIES RULE! sticker on it to tell that it was Tori's.

Tori looked, as usual, completely unrepentant. "No harm done, chief," she said. "I mean, sir. Just trying to speed up in the traffic between classes."

"You can't skateboard in the halls, Tori. Troy Marcus is coming to visit in just a few more days, and we can't have you knocking him down." Mr.

Picture Perfect?

Merlin was trying to sound mad, but you could tell he was trying not to smile. *For an assistant principal,* Lara thought, *Mr. Merlin really is pretty nice.*

"Hello, Lara," Mr. Merlin said. He handed Tori back her skateboard. "Have a good lunch, girls . . . and walk to the cafeteria, if you please."

Tori laughed after Mr. Merlin moved away down the hall. "Proper ear-bashing I was getting. Thanks for coming by at the right moment to rescue me."

Lara felt better already. Tori's English was crazier than Lara's, but she was so much fun to listen to, Lara didn't mind guessing what she meant half the time.

"Want to split some chocolate with me?" she asked.

"Would I?" Tori said. "Lead the way!"

In the cafeteria, Tori and Lara sorted through Grandmama's goodie box.

"Your grandma is aces, Lara!" Tori said, biting into a chocolate truffle. "My family practically never sends me chocolate except on my birthday." She chuckled, "Actually the folks had a *major blue* about chocolate once."

"A what?" Lara asked.

"A fight, you know," Tori explained. "Dad forgot to give Mum chocolate for their anniversary, and she had a fit! Loves chocolate, my mum."

"Your parents argue?" Lara sighed with relief internally. She hadn't even had to bring it up.

"Sure! It doesn't mean anything, though. They wouldn't know what to do without each other. They're like two pieces of a puzzle even when they're yelling. Your folks the same way?"

"Sometimes," Lara said with a shrug. Now that she knew that Tori's parents fought, too, she felt a little better. And talking about how bad it made her feel just made her sound like a baby. She could handle it. "But I think I will just ignore it."

"Best thing to do," Tori said, rooting through her backpack. "How's the art project going?"

"Almost done," Lara said. "I have to add the final touches on the paintings, then it is finished!"

"Bonzer! So what will you do with all that cash?"

"I have to win first, Tori," said Lara. "I think half the young artists in New York City are entering the competition."

"Ha! You've got it all sewn up, as far as I'm concerned. Where's the actual contest?"

Picture Perfect?

"They're clearing out a gallery at the famous Metropolitan Museum of Art for the exhibits of the finalists. If I make the finals."

"*Cor!*" Tori whistled. "Wouldn't that be something if you got a painting hung at the Met? Your parents would go nuts!"

Lara nodded, wishing Tori hadn't mentioned her parents. It brought back the worries she'd been trying to ignore all day. Tori had said her own parents were like two pieces of the same puzzle, even when they were fighting. But Lara's mama and papa? They were like pieces of two totally different puzzles, even when they weren't arguing at all.

The two girls walked up the stairs to the fifth floor to dump their books in their lockers. On the way back, Lara checked the loose floor tile for a note. She and Tori had discovered the tile by accident during the first week of school, and the hidden space beneath it had become a perfect secret message center for all their friends. Lara saw a purple note with her name written on it. Barbie had beautiful pink stationery, so it wasn't from her. It had to be from Nichelle, who had a total craze for everything purple.

Sure enough, it was from Nichelle. The note said:

Dear Lara,
Hey, there, girl! Haven't seen a lot of you these days, art goddess. (Remember us when you're rich and famous!) This Troy Marcus madness is so out of hand, I'm practically sorry Chelsie talked me into being on the Welcoming Committee. Do you want to drop the paintbrush for a minute and grab a soda and some fries tomorrow after school? Write back soon and let me know.

Love,
Nichelle

Lara tore off a piece of her own stationery pad, with her favorite Paris hotel's logo at the top, and dashed off a quick reply.

Dear Nichelle,
For you, I'd drop the brush anytime! And I would love your advice on my art project, too, before I turn it in to the committee. Meet you on the front steps at 3:00 tomorrow?

Ciao,
Lara

Picture Perfect?

She folded the note, wrote Nichelle's name on the outside, and dropped it into the space under the tile. Then she shoved the tile back into place, without a seam showing. E-mail might be faster, but the tile was way more fun. It made the long, long walk up the stairs to the fifth-floor lockers almost bearable.

But after that, nothing went right the whole rest of the day. Barbie had to ask her a question three times before Lara heard her, and she gave Lara kind of a strange look before they separated to go to different classes. Even though her feelings were a little hurt, Lara tried to make Barbie feel better by laughing and saying that it was just the sugar from all the chocolate she'd eaten. She said the same thing to Ms. Gortney, her physics teacher, when she messed up her experiment for the third time.

Lara bolted for the subway as soon as class was over. She just wanted to get out of I. H. today and start over fresh tomorrow, as if the whole day had never happened.

Chapter 6

It Can't Be True!

Lara climbed the steps of the subway, two blocks from her loft. She was already feeling a tiny bit better. Mama and Papa would end this silly fight, whatever it was about, and then things would go back to normal. She just had to ignore it, as she'd told Tori, and everything would be fine. She opened the door of the loft with her key, hoping nobody was home. She didn't hear voices, thank goodness.

But when she went inside, Mama and Papa were both waiting for her at the kitchen table. Neither one said anything, and then they both spoke at once.

Picture Perfect?

"*Liebchen*, we've been waiting to talk to you," Papa said.

Mama said, at the same instant, "Lara, my darling, you're finally home."

They both broke off, awkwardly looking at each other and then back at Lara.

"What on earth is going on?" Lara was so flustered, she didn't even realize she'd said this out loud.

Finally, after another long, awkward silence, Mama answered. But it wasn't really an answer at all. "Lara, you know your father and I have not been getting along these days."

Papa broke in. "It has nothing to do with you, *liebchen*. We both love you, my dearest child."

Mama said, "It's just that your Papa and I are so different from each other, we . . ." She stretched her hands out to Lara as if she wanted to hug her, but dropped them. "I don't know what to say to her, Friedrich," Mama said to Papa.

"And you think I do, Lucia?" Papa said, his head in his hands. "Sit down, Lara."

Lara said sharply, "No, I don't want to." Lara was shocked at herself. She never spoke to Papa like that. But she didn't want to sit down with them.

She wanted to run right out the door before she heard another word.

Papa wasn't angry at Lara, though. He just patted the seat next to his. Lara sank into it, feeling sick to her stomach.

Mama took Lara's hand and held it in her own. "Your father and I need to live apart for a little while, *carina*."

Lara's whole world rocked around her. It was all she could do not to burst out crying.

"But, but . . ." Lara choked out the words, and then a tear rolled down her face.

Papa put both his arms around her instantly. "I won't be far away, Lara. Only a few blocks away, in faculty housing at NYU."

"You're leaving!" Lara shrieked at Papa. "How can you leave me?"

Mama put a hand over her mouth, and the color drained from her face. She reached out for Lara again, but Lara pulled back from her. "Are you making Papa leave? Are you? How can you do this?"

"It is easier for me to leave because of the faculty housing, *liebchen*," Papa said, sounding utterly miserable.

"Easier? Easier for whom?" Lara cried. "Not me." She stood up. "Neither one of you cares about me at all!"

"Lara!" Mama said. "That isn't true! We love you more than anything."

But Lara wasn't listening. "Well, let's just make it universal! I'm leaving, too!"

Lara grabbed her keys and ran out the door and down the stairs, heading for the street. Mama and Papa were so shocked, they just sat there for a second before leaping up to go after her, but they were too slow. Lara was down the stairs and outside before they even got out the door of the loft.

They are probably right behind me, Lara thought as she made it to the street. She almost decided to stop and let them catch her. Her world was ruined, anyway, so what did it matter? She could never make it all the way to the subway station ahead of them. But, as if she were in a movie, a cab pulled up right in front of her just at that moment.

Lara hailed the cab and climbed in, feeling as if she was in a nightmare. She'd never taken a cab in New York without her parents. But the cabdriver didn't care.

"Where to, kid?"

"Please, take me to International High School as fast as you can," she said in a voice thick with tears. The cab pulled away with a screech of tires. She thought she heard Papa shout her name from behind the cab, but she didn't turn her head to look back.

In the cab, Lara put her head in her hands. They'd lived all over the world together, but they were always a family! What were they now? Nothing! Utterly nothing!

She got out of the cab in front of the school and started to walk away. The cabdriver cleared his throat. "Look, Miss, I'm not running a public charity here, okay?" He held his hand out. "You owe me eight-fifty."

Lara searched all her pockets. She hadn't even thought about money; she'd just wanted to get away. Finally, with the cabdriver getting more and more frustrated, Lara found a ten-dollar bill wadded up in the pocket of her jacket and gave it to him.

He counted out her change and handed it to her. She said, "No, keep it for a tip."

"You hang on to it, kid. I got kids of my own, and you shouldn't be out without any money at all. At least this way you got enough to call someone." He rolled up his window and pulled away.

Lara walked up to the front door of I. H. and tugged on it. Locked! Oh, that was just perfect. And since she'd left her purse back at the loft, she didn't even have her subway pass to get her home. And she certainly wasn't going to call her parents to come and get her. She just had to get into the school! She peered in through the glass door, trying to spot someone to open it for her.

Suddenly she saw Poogy in the hallway. She pounded frantically on the door to attract his attention. But he was walking away from the door, not toward it. She pounded harder. He had to hear her, he just had to. Finally, just as he was about to turn the corner and go out of sight, he turned around.

He walked back and pushed the door open to talk to Lara, but wouldn't let her in. "We close early today for the construction repairs," Poogy said. "Didn't you hear Principal Simmons's announcement?"

Lara said desperately, "I have to get my book. I left it up on the fifth floor. I won't be long. Please, Poogy, I won't get in the way."

He studied Lara's face. "Okay, okay, don't get so

upset. You're a good kid. Come on in and get your book. But stay out of the way," he cautioned.

"I will," Lara promised.

He opened up the door to let Lara in and locked it behind her. "You go out the side door when you leave, through the student tunnel. The main doors are all locked up," Poogy directed.

Lara took a deep breath, looking around at the empty corridors of the school, the walls still plastered with Troy Marcus posters. Then she started the long climb up to the fifth floor.

On the way upstairs, Lara remembered something. She kept an emergency five-dollar bill in her locker, to use if she forgot her lunch money. And if there was ever an emergency, this was it!

She opened her locker on the first try, for once, and found the five-dollar bill. Now what? It was as though her brain had stopped working. She sat down on the floor in front of her open locker and cried.

Finally she scrubbed her face with the old wadded-up art smock in her locker. Much as she wanted to, she couldn't stay here all night. But what could she do?

She could call one of her friends!

Picture Perfect?

Lara jumped to her feet. Sweet-natured Barbie, sassy Tori, independent Nichelle, practical Ana, sensitive Chelsie — one of them would know what she should do. They'd come to the school and help her. But she sank back down again on one of the plastic chairs by the fifth-floor pay phone. She couldn't do it. She pictured picking up the phone, talking to Barbie, or to Nichelle, or to Tori. *"My parents are getting separated,"* she said in her mind. *"Papa's moving out and leaving me behind."* She couldn't say it out loud. If she said it out loud, then it was really true. She knew that was silly, that it was true no matter what, but that was how she felt. Yet she had to do something or she would just go crazy.

How could she tell someone if she couldn't say it? Then she remembered the tile's hiding place. She could write a note to everyone, explaining the situation. She was supposed to meet Nichelle tomorrow after school, anyway. The other girls would come, too, if she invited them. Lara thought she could probably get the words out by tomorrow. For now, she could just write notes. Her friends would get them tomorrow whenever they checked under the tile.

She found an empty classroom that still had its

door unlocked, and sat down to write. The note was short and to the point. Lara knew she had never been very good at expressing her feelings in words. Kind of like Papa. She angrily wiped more tears out of her eyes. Papa was leaving! She wasn't crying for him, or for Mama, either. She wrote Nichelle's note first, since she was supposed to meet her tomorrow.

Dear Nichelle,
HELP! I think my parents are getting a divorce. My father is moving out to faculty housing. I'm so upset, I don't know who I can count on except my friends. Please meet me at 3:00 on the front steps the way we planned. I don't know what to do, and I need advice really badly, so I'm writing notes to the other girls, too. Thanks for being my friend.

Love,
Lara

She studied the words on the paper for a long minute, particularly the word "divorce." The note wasn't great, but it would have to do. She wrote similar notes to everyone else. *Meet me at 3:00,* she said in all of them. *I need your help!*

Picture Perfect?

Finally, she was done. The sky outside the window had darkened into night. She folded each note, checking to make sure each girl's name was on the outside. Then she went back out into the hallway and put them all under the tile.

She felt shaky and exhausted, but at least she had done something. Her friends would come through for her tomorrow. Now she could go home.

She passed Poogy on the stairs as she was walking down to leave.

"That must have been some heavy book you had to get," Poogy said.

"It was. You are working late, too, aren't you?"

"Lots of overtime for me, yes." He smiled. "Fixing up the school for the big movie star." He walked past her up the stairs, carrying his tools.

Lara ran downstairs and out the side door. She had to get home. Her parents would be frantic by now.

* * * *

Poogy continued all the way up to the fifth floor. He talked to himself as he went. "I'll be so happy, they get that escalator fixed. Big movie star has to be good for something." He stopped halfway down the fifth-floor hallway. "Huh," he said, noticing a loose tile in the floor. He nudged the girls' message tile with his foot. There was a tiny gap between the tile and the rest of the floor, where Lara had forgotten to shove the tile all the way back into place.

He pulled out a tube of epoxy glue from his toolbox, squirted it thickly all around the edges of the tile, and held it in place. "Once this dries," he said out loud, "this tile will never come loose."

Chapter 7

Nobody Cares!

Lara woke up the following morning, curled up on her air mattress at the loft. For a brief moment, as she stretched in the sunlight, she forgot everything that had happened. But it all came back to her in a rush of memory that made her feel sick. Her parents were separating, maybe even getting a divorce.

Last night, when she came back, Mama and Papa had both been waiting for her. She'd thought they were going to yell at her for running away like that, but they hadn't.

Papa had blamed himself, "Ach, *liebchen*, ve never should have sprung it on you like that. Ve

67

looked and looked for you. But ve didn't have any of your friends' phone numbers to call you. Ve called the school, but the office was closed for construction."

Mama had said, "We just didn't know how to tell you. I've been going crazy with worry the past few months about this, and so has Papa."

Lara had cried out, "Why didn't you tell me? Why did you pretend everything was okay? It only made it worse!"

Papa had put his hand on her shoulder, "Ve should have, Lara. Ve thought ve could make it work, but ve can't right now."

Mama had said, "It doesn't mean we won't keep trying. We've been together for sixteen years, *carina*. We just need to be apart for a while."

Lara had felt so exhausted suddenly, she'd almost couldn't stand. Swaying with tiredness, she'd told her parents, "I can't think about this anymore tonight."

Mama had said, "Go to sleep, baby. Sleep late; you don't need to go to school tomorrow if you don't want. I'll write you a note." She'd kissed Lara. "Remember that your father and I both love you so much. Nothing changes that."

Picture Perfect?

Papa had kissed her, too. "Your mother is right. We'll talk in the morning, *liebchen*."

Lara had staggered up the ladder to her studio, collapsed on her air mattress with her shoes and school clothes still on, and fallen fast asleep.

Now it was morning, and Lara lay very still, trying to hear if her parents were awake. No noise at all came from the rest of the loft. The sunlight was pouring in the windows. It had to be really late for it to be so sunny and bright. Lara peeped at the clock by her bed. It was 11:30 A.M. She had already missed three classes! Lara sat up, dumping her sheets into a pile on the floor, and looked over the side of the platform.

Mama was asleep sitting up in the living room armchair. Papa was asleep, too, collapsed on the couch. They both looked exhausted. They'd probably stayed up all night.

Lara tiptoed down the ladder. She got two blankets out of the linen closet. Just because she was angry at them didn't mean she was going to let them catch a cold. She draped one blanket over Mama, and one over Papa. Neither one of them woke up, which was fine with Lara. She needed more time to think before she talked to them again.

Lara got ready for school quickly, pulling clothes that weren't too wrinkled out of the dirty laundry hamper. The closet door where her clean clothes hung squeaked too loudly, and she didn't want the noise to wake them. Papa had been meaning to oil it for months, but he hadn't gotten around to it. *Guess he never will, now.* Lara felt shocked by the thought. Papa wouldn't live here anymore. What would that be like?

She glanced around the loft. All of their furniture was theirs, the whole family's, not just Mama's or just Papa's. The armchair the family had bought in Paris. The painting Lara had picked out in Milan. The bookcase that took Mama and Papa five hours to put together because it only had directions in Japanese. How could they divide up their lives?

Mama stirred in the armchair. Lara froze. Was she waking up?

But Mama just pulled the blanket tighter around herself without waking up. Papa snored loudly. Lara tiptoed into the kitchen. She needed paper and a pen from the telephone table. But what to write?

Finally she settled on the wording for her note.

Picture Perfect?

Dear Mama and Papa,
I have gone to meet my friend Nichelle after school.
Do not worry about me. I will be home before dark,
and we can talk more then.

Love,
Lara

The beat-up antique telephone table in the kitchen had bright green and yellow paint spots splotched all over the legs. Lara had painted them herself when she was only four years old, with the first real set of paints she ever got. She'd gotten in big trouble when Grandmama had caught her merrily splashing paint all over the wood as high as her four-year-old hands could reach. *I wonder who'll get the telephone table. Mama or Papa?* Tears welled up again, and she blew her nose quietly in a paper towel. She had to get out of there, right now.

Lara ran down the stairs to the street. It was so strange to be out in the city in the middle of the afternoon on a school day. No other teenagers were out and about. Under other circumstances, it might have been fun.

Suddenly she wondered about the notes she'd

left at school. At least Tori, Barbie, and Nichelle would have read their notes by now. She knew they checked the tile at least twice a day. And Ana and Chelsie checked it every afternoon between classes. What would they be thinking? They'd probably be worried sick when they saw she wasn't in class. They would all be wondering what to do. It made her feel a little better knowing that her friends all cared about her, even when the rest of her world was falling apart. She could count on them, even if she couldn't count on her parents.

It was almost 1:00 in the afternoon, Lara realized. Should she go to school now? Or just wait? She'd already been marked absent by now, so there wasn't much point. She couldn't handle sitting in class and pretending everything was fine. Nothing was ever going to be fine again. Even the New Artists' Competition didn't feel like it mattered anymore.

Lara decided what to do. She would go to school at 2:30, in time to meet everyone at 3:00. But what would she do until then? As if to answer her, her stomach rumbled. She would get something to eat.

Picture Perfect?

* * * *

Back at school, Tori and Nichelle were talking in the hallway between classes.

"Have you seen Lara?" Nichelle asked, lacing up her purple high-top sneakers.

"No mate, not all day," Tori said. "Maybe she's sick or something. Oh, wait. Maybe she's just holed up in the art studio to finish her art project. It's due on Friday." She slung her leather jacket over her shoulder.

"I was supposed to meet her at three o'clock to talk about her art project, so maybe that's it," Nichelle said. "I think it was three o'clock, anyway." She pulled Lara's now-rumpled note out of her pocket to check the time. "'Dear Nichelle,'" she read, "'for you, I'd drop the brush anytime! And I would love your advice on my art project, too, before I turn it in to the committee. Meet you on the front steps at 3:00 tomorrow?'"

"But I'm not going to have very much time as it turns out," Nichelle went on. "Chelsie's moved the Welcome Troy Marcus Committee meeting to three-fifteen today, and since I'm cochair, well . . ."

"Lara will understand," Tori said. "Leave her a note upstairs. She checks the tile all the time."

"That's the problem! I wrote a note to her and tried to put it upstairs. But" — Nichelle paused for effect — "the tile is cemented shut!"

"What?" Tori was outraged. "Who would do that?"

"I don't know. Maybe somebody saw us and reported it." Nichelle shrugged. "It's no biggie. We'll find some other spot for messages."

"Yeah, but it still rots, if you ask me," Tori said.

"I know," Nichelle said ruefully. "But what can we do?"

"Hi, guys," Barbie said, dropping her books on the bench as she sat down. "What are you guys doing after school?"

"Just call me committee woman," Nichelle said ruefully. "You know how I overcommit myself. I was supposed to hang with Lara and chat about her art project, but such is life. Can either of you go with Lara instead?"

"Love to, but no can do," Tori said. "I'm going skateboarding with the Pants Boys. Way more fun than some staid old meeting!"

Barbie said, "I wish I could go hang out with Lara today. Her art project is totally awesome! But

Picture Perfect?

I'm going shopping for a birthday present for my little sister. By the way," she added, "where is Lara, anyway? I haven't seen her all day."

"We aren't sure. Probably working on her art project," Nichelle said. "Tori was saying that it's due on Friday."

Barbie sighed with relief. "That makes sense. I've been kind of worried about Lara. She's been a little out of it the past few weeks. It's not like her. But it's probably just because she's so focused on the art thing." Barbie reassured Nichelle, "She'll understand about the meeting, Nichelle. One more day won't make any difference."

* * * *

Back in SoHo, Lara was finishing her lunch at the pizzeria near the subway. After a greasy slice of pizza and a soda, she hopped on the train to go to school. She was desperate to see her friends. They would help her.

At West Street, Lara ran through the student tunnel, flashing her student ID to the security guard. It was almost 3:00 already, and she had to get to the front steps. She pushed her way through the crowd of students streaming outside and took the shortcut to the front lobby.

She peered around people, searching for Nichelle. There she was! Nichelle stood on the front steps, dressed in jeans, a pink T-shirt, and purple high-tops.

"Oh, Nichelle, I am so glad to see you!" Lara said. "Did you get my note?"

"Sure thing, Lara, and lucky I got it when I did!" Nichelle said offhandedly, looking at her watch.

Lara slowed to a halt. This was kind of an odd response. And what did Nichelle mean she was lucky to get it when she did? Nichelle had never been so uncaring. Lara had expected a big hug. And where were the others?

Nichelle said, "Look, Lara, I know you said you wanted my advice today. I feel really bad, but I have to reschedule, okay?"

"Reschedule?" Lara choked. "But —"

"You know how it is. Chelsie moved up the Welcome Troy Marcus Committee meeting. Your stuff can wait until tomorrow, right?"

"Chelsie won't come, either?" Lara asked in a small voice.

Nichelle looked puzzled. "Well, no. You know

76

how important the Troy Marcus thing is to her. Not like your thing isn't super important to her, too, but the meeting is right now. I'm sure she'll look in on you later. Maybe tomorrow."

"And Barbie? Tori? Ana?"

"Barbie wanted to come, she really did, but she had to go shopping. And Tori had skateboarding plans, so she told me to tell you she'd catch you later. I think Ana's studying with Blaine."

Lara just stared. This couldn't be happening!

Nichelle laughed, patting Lara on the shoulder. "You shouldn't take this so seriously, Lara. You really look exhausted." She said, "Just remember, there's no point in stressing about it one way or the other. In a few days, the whole thing will be all over, am I right? It'll be fine."

She glanced at her watch again. "Argh! I have to run, or Chelsie will kick my rear. I'll catch you later, okay?"

Before Lara could even say a single word, Nichelle was gone.

Lara couldn't believe it. They didn't care about her at all! Her world was falling apart, and her friends were going shopping? *I am nothing to them!* her mind shrieked. *Nothing!*

Lara pushed back in through the school doors and ran blindly for the art studio. She collided heavily with Poogy the janitor, almost knocking him to the floor.

"Sorry, Poogy," Lara cried, running past him without stopping.

Poogy shook his head in amazement. He'd always thought of Lara as a very levelheaded girl. But this was the second day in a row he'd seen her crying her eyes out.

Lara crashed through the doorway into the empty art studio on the third floor. With wild eyes, she stared at her paintings of Rainbow House and the Statue of Liberty. The unfinished figure of the girl standing on the deck of the ferry, staring up into the rain, called to her. She knew who that lost-looking girl was now. All alone in the world, nobody to care for her. It was her! She snatched up a brush and began to paint furiously.

When Lara was done, she threw the paintbrush down on the table without even rinsing it. What difference did it make if the brush was ruined? She ran from the room.

Rain was falling outside the school as Lara walked, and she didn't have a raincoat. But why should she care about that? Her whole world had changed beyond recognition. Everything she'd ever believed was all a lie, anyway. Her friends were not her friends. Her parents were getting a divorce.

Lara walked and walked, until her shoes were full of icy water from all the puddles she'd stepped in. Finally, she was at the harbor. The ferry loomed before her. She used the last of her money to buy a ticket and walked on board. She sat down on a coil of rope up in the bow of the boat and watched the waves.

Chapter 8

Where's Lara?

Nichelle sat in the "Welcome Troy Marcus" Committee meeting, tapping her pencil on the table and feeling uncomfortable. Lara had looked awfully upset. Maybe Nichelle could have blown off this meeting, or at least shown up late. She promised herself that she would go find Lara first thing, as soon as the meeting was over. She looked at her watch. Four-fifteen already?

The door creaked open a little bit, and Barbie snuck into the meeting, sitting down in the back of the room. She was carrying a Macy's shopping bag, so Nichelle figured she must have found a gift for her little sister. She was also carrying a bright red umbrella.

Tori was there, too. She was dripping wet, puddles forming underneath her chair. Even Tori couldn't skateboard in the rain! Ana came in behind Barbie, plunking down a mammoth stack of books.

Nichelle felt better. The minute this silly meeting was over, they could all go find Lara together. She was probably just holed up in the art studio on the third floor. If she was stressing about the art competition, the least they could do was take her out for an ice-cream sundae and a movie.

Finally, Chelsie asked, "does anyone else have anything to add?" Thank goodness, nobody did. "Then I officially declare the meeting over. We'll meet again for the last time at lunchtime on Thursday. Friday's the big day, people, so let's make it a great one."

There was a spatter of applause, and then the meeting was over. Nichelle said, "Great job, Chelsie."

"Thanks," Chelsie said. "Hey, looks like everybody's here."

"Everyone except Lara," Barbie said, looking around. "Where is she?"

Nichelle said, "I think she's freaking out about her art project a little. How about we go find her and pump her up a little?"

Tori said, "That's kind of unlike her. Lara doesn't stress!"

Barbie said, "Maybe that's why we didn't notice it. We're so used to thinking of her as having the perfect life, we don't think she even can stress out! I think she's been acting funny for weeks."

Ana said, "Hey, it can happen to everyone. Remember me before the triathlon? Let's go find her right now. Does anyone know where she is?"

Barbie said, "The art studio's on the third floor."

Nichelle said, "Then what are we waiting for? Let's go!"

The girls piled on the escalators up to the art studio room. But the door was locked! Tori and Nichelle pounded on it, just in case Lara was inside. Barbie peered through the frosted glass. "I don't think anyone's in there," she said uncertainly.

Ana called, "Lara! It's us — open the door." No answer.

Chelsie said, "I feel so bad. I've been so

obsessed with Troy, I didn't even think about Lara at all."

Poogy came down the hallway. "You looking for Lara?"

"Yes, we sure are," Barbie said. "Have you seen her?"

Poogy scratched his head, "Crying today, crying last night. What's the matter with her?"

Tori was astounded. "Lara? Crying? Are you sure you have the right girl? Dark hair, green eyes, always covered in paint. That Lara?"

Poogy nodded. "Crying so hard last night, up on the fifth floor. And she almost knocked me down today after school, running away from something."

"When I told her I had to reschedule our meeting!" Nichelle smacked her forehead. "I am so stupid. But how could I know she was having a major freak-out?"

Barbie said, "Hang on, Poogy. Lara was crying last night?" She turned to Nichelle, "That couldn't have been about your meeting."

"Up on the fifth floor," Poogy said. "Writing many little notes and crying. She was so upset, she didn't even know I was up there dumping the trash."

"Little notes? Oh, no!" Nichelle said. She turned to Barbie. "When I met Lara on the steps today, she asked me if I got her note. And I said yes. But what if she wrote a brand-new note last night?"

Barbie said, "Poogy, we need to borrow some of your tools."

"What for? I can't just give you tools."

"Poogy, I promise it's an emergency. We'll return them in perfect shape!"

"Okay, but only 'cause I know you're good girls. Here, take what you need." He offered his toolbox.

Tori grabbed a hammer and a screwdriver. "Thanks Poogie," she said.

The girls ran up the last two flights to the fifth floor.

"Hurry up, Tori," Ana demanded. "Get the tile open."

Tori pried at it, but the epoxy glue held it firmly in place.

"Come on, Tori!" Barbie said. "Lara's depending on us."

Finally, the tile popped free. Tori wiped sweat from her face.

"Is there anything in there?" Chelsie said anxiously.

"Yeah," Tori said. "There's a note for each of us." She passed them out. Then she put the tile back in place so the girls could use it again for messages later.

"Oh, no," Barbie said as she read. "Poor Lara! Her parents are getting divorced?"

Nichelle looked stricken. "Oh, this is terrible. She thinks we all got these notes! And she thinks we care more about meetings and shopping and skateboarding than we do about her!"

"We have to find her!" Tori said.

"But, where?" Ana said. "She could be anywhere in New York!"

"She was going to the art studio when Poogy saw her, right?" said Barbie.

Chelsie said, "Maybe she left a note or something in there about where she went."

The girls all ran downstairs again. The art studio door now stood wide open. "Lara!" Chelsie shouted.

But it was just Poogy, who was looking at all the paintings as he was mopping the floor. "That Lara can paint," he said, looking at the Statute of Liberty harbor painting. "Looks just like the real thing, but better."

The girls started searching the room for clues. They looked at every scrap of paper, but there wasn't a hint of where Lara had gone. What were they going to do?

Poogy went on, "And this painted girl standing on the ferry looks just like her!"

"What did you say?" Barbie asked. The girls gathered around the painting on the easel. It was true! Lara had painted herself on the deck of the ferry.

Nichelle breathed a sigh. "I bet that's where she is."

"Let's go!" Barbie said urgently.

"Thanks a million, Poogy!" Tori said as they ran out of the room.

"And, Poogy?" Nichelle shouted back over her shoulder. "Can you do us a favor and leave that tile on the fifth floor loose?"

"Okey-dokey," they heard the mystified Poogy say.

Outside the school, the girls slowed down in confusion.

"Should we take the subway?" Chelsie asked.

"It'll take too long!" Nichelle said. "Let's all split a cab."

Picture Perfect?

The five girls squashed into a cab, ignoring a glare from the driver. "Take us to the Staten Island Ferry, please, as fast as you can!" Barbie said, and with a squeal of tires, they were off.

The cab rocketed over potholes, shaking the girls as if they were pinballs. Tori hit her head on the roof of the cab so hard, she saw stars. "Crikey, our cabdriver's mental!"

"As long as he gets us there in one piece," Ana said, hanging on to the back of the seat.

At last, the ferry pickup point loomed up ahead of them. The smell of salt water filled the air, and a cold breeze whipped around their ankles. The rain had almost stopped, but it was still drizzling.

Nichelle shivered as the girls paid the cabdriver. "What if she's not here?"

"Then we'll look till we find her somewhere else," Barbie said firmly. "We're not giving up."

"There's the ferry," Chelsie shouted, pointing out into the harbor. It was coming slowly toward them.

They hopped on, and in a few minutes it pulled out again. Usually the ferry was packed, but today the rain had driven away most of the tourist crowds. A few people huddled dismally under raincoats, warming their hands on cups of hot chocolate. No Lara! A flight of metal stairs led up to the second level. Nichelle said, "I'll check upstairs." But there was no one upstairs at all.

"Oh, where can she be?" Barbie said, wringing her hands. "Excuse me, sir," Barbie said to a passing crew member. "Is there someplace else a passenger could be? We're looking for a friend."

"She could be standing out front on the bow. She'd be crazy to do it in this weather, though."

It was true. The rain had started coming down again in sheets. Surely Lara wouldn't be out there in weather like this. But Barbie braced herself to go look, anyway, even if it was just the smallest chance.

She opened her red umbrella. "I'm going to look outside."

As she went out, the force of the storm instantly turned her umbrella inside out. The rain soaked her. This was nuts! But then Barbie saw a huddled figure at the railing. "Lara?" she called out.

The figure turned around. It was Lara! She wasn't even wearing a raincoat, and her beautiful dark hair hung dripping around her face.

* * * *

88

Picture Perfect?

Lara was shivering at the rail of the ferry when she heard Barbie's voice. She spun around to face Barbie, eyes stinging with tears. "All done with the shopping?" she said bitterly. "Finally do you have the time in your busy life for Lara?"

"Oh, Lara!" Barbie said despairingly. "We didn't know! None of us got your notes because the school cemented the tile down."

Could it be true? Lara felt a moment of doubt. She wasn't forgiving the people who broke her heart that easily. She said, "Nichelle said she did get my note. You were all just too busy for my problems!"

Barbie shook her head. "Nichelle thought you meant the other note, the one talking about your painting. Everybody would have been there to help you if they'd only known. How long have you been out here?" Barbie draped her coat over Lara's shoulders.

"It felt like hours. I didn't know where else to go." Her teeth were chattering from the cold. Had it all just been a horrible misunderstanding? "I needed you, and I mattered to none of you!" Lara yelled angrily. Then she burst into tears.

"Lara —" Barbie broke off, not knowing what to

say to her friend. Lara had always been the strong one, who never needed any help. So when she had really needed it, no one had even noticed. "If we had only known!"

"You mean you really do care about me?" Lara asked in a whisper.

"Of course we do! Everybody's here right now. Come on inside, and they'll tell you themselves."

And that's what they did. Nichelle shouted with relief when Barbie and Lara came in, and all the girls gathered around her.

Nichelle took off her purple knit scarf and wrapped it around Lara's neck. "Lara, if I'd only known, I'd never have gone to that stupid meeting. You have to believe me!"

"You're much more important than some movie star, even if it is Troy Marcus," Chelsie said. "I would have canceled the whole thing in a second."

"Yeah," Tori agreed. "Did you really think I thought skateboarding was more important than you? Never for a minute, mate!" She shook Lara's arm. "We're your friends!"

Ana handed Lara a cup full of steaming hot chocolate. "Drink this and tell us everything that happened with your parents."

Picture Perfect?

Lara poured out the whole story, right there on the ferry. Her friends sat around her, supporting her, just the way she had known they would. It was still terrible and scary. But at least she had friends she could count on. And that made all the difference in the world.

Chapter 9

Hooray for Hollywood?

Lara met Chelsie and Barbie before class on Friday. Today was the big day! The school had been crawling with Troy's publicists all week. They'd been snapping pictures, picking camera angles, and putting up even more Troy Marcus posters. Finally, his head publicist had arrived. She was a young woman, in jeans and a blouse, bursting with energy. "Hi, I'm Marie Chung. Which one of you is Chelsie?"

"I am," Chelsie said nervously. She had agonized over what to wear all week, and she'd finally settled on a pretty yellow cotton dress and short black boots.

"It is so good to meet you!" Marie shook Chelsie's hand. "I was so impressed with the letter you sent. It's wonderful that you and your friends do so much volunteer work at the homeless shelter. That's why I — I mean Troy — picked your letter." She went on, "Did you like the roses?"

"They were great! But I thought Troy sent them?"

"Uh . . ." Marie paused, and then smiled at Chelsie. "Sort of." She went on, "I have to warn you guys, Troy is pretty busy. He won't have a whole lot of time to be social."

A news crew was setting up their cameras in the hallway. "Where do you want us, Ms. Chung?"

Marie directed them down the hall to the front steps, where Principal Simmons was going to present the key to the school to Troy Marcus. A platform with a podium on it had been set up so all the camera crews could get a great view. A canvas screen created a tiny "backstage" where Marie could stand out of sight with the sound engineers. "Okay, girls, he'll be here any minute."

Suddenly, a black stretch limo pulled up. The chauffeur opened the back door of the car, and Troy Marcus stepped out. Flashbulbs were popping all around.

"Oh, it's him, it's really him!" Chelsie said.

"I know, can you believe it?" Nichelle said, poking Lara in the side. "Check him out, girl."

Lara smiled. It was still tough for her to really care about some movie star, compared to what was going on in her life. But it was great seeing how thrilled her friends were! "*Oui*, he is gorgeous."

Chelsie squeezed Lara's hand. Even in the middle of all the excitement, Chelsie was keeping Lara close at hand. Ever since the note mix-up, Chelsie and Lara had become closer friends than ever.

Tori strained her neck to see Troy. "Bonzer! And he's our principal all day long."

Ana said, "Yeah, send me to the principal's office right this minute."

Marie waded across the crowd and grabbed Chelsie's other hand. "He wants the girl who invited him to hand him the key. You're on, kid."

Chelsie said, "In front of all those cameras?" She clutched nervously at Lara, who was standing closest to her. "Come with me, okay?"

Picture Perfect?

Suddenly the two girls were standing backstage with Marie. The press conference would start any minute. Lara reassured Chelsie for the tenth time that her hair looked great. And then Troy Marcus was there with them in the tiny backstage space. He looked right at Chelsie and put his hand on her shoulder. Lara thought Chelsie might faint on the spot!

Troy began to speak, in the famous voice Lara had last heard from the movie screen. Chelsie smiled up at him dreamily.

"Marie, couldn't you have found a better dress for this kid?" Troy said. "You know I look terrible anywhere near the color yellow! Get some other kid to give me the key, will you? Somebody better dressed!" Troy's voice was still deep, but it had a whining note Lara had never noticed in his movies.

"She's the one who invited you, Troy, remember?" Marie sounded worn out.

"You think my fans care about that? They're here to see me, not her, okay? I have to look good. Ixnay on the yellow!"

"Honey," Marie said to Chelsie, "I'll be right back. Don't you even move. I'll fix this."

Lara just watched in horror. Chelsie couldn't

have moved even if she'd wanted to. Troy Marcus was Chelsie's hero! She'd seen every movie he'd ever made at least five times. Had he really been so creepy?

Marie came back through the crowd carrying a dark blue sweater. It was Barbie's, Lara realized. "I borrowed this from one of your friends, Chelsie," Marie whispered. "Throw this on over the dress. Troy won't even notice as long as he thinks we've done something."

Marie saw Chelsie's face, eyes brimming with tears. She put an arm around her. "Don't you listen to him, Chelsie. He's just fussy about colors from being on camera all the time. It doesn't mean a thing."

"Can we start now?" Troy said impatiently. "I can't stand around all day!" He went on, "Somebody hand me the stupid rose, will you? I don't know whose idea the rose was, but if I get one more thorn in my finger, the person working props is going to be looking for a new job!"

Marie kept a professional smile on her face, but the girls could tell her nerves were fraying. "The thorns were all removed, Troy. I checked the rose personally."

Picture Perfect?

"Okay, kid," said Troy, leaning over Chelsie. "Remember, they're here to see me, not you, so don't get in my light. You hand me the key, I hand you the rose. You smile and look awestruck. Got it?"

Chelsie didn't say anything. Lara could see her swallowing back tears.

"Oh, give me a break, Marie," Troy said. "Can this girl talk, or is she just not getting it?"

Marie interrupted, "She gets it, she gets it. It'll be fine. Looks like everyone's ready, Chelsie." She squeezed Chelsie's arm and whispered in her ear, "Ignore him, he's just being a jerk. I thought your dress looked great. Now get out there and knock 'em dead."

Chelsie stood backstage in a daze, holding the big ceremonial gold key she'd picked out as the head of the Welcome Committee. Lara held her hand tightly. *Maybe this is just the way things are out in Hollywood,* Lara thought. *Troy probably didn't really mean any of those mean things he said.*

As if to prove the point, Troy Marcus swept out onto the platform. He looked just the way he did in all his movies: Dashing good looks and a beautiful smile. He aimed that smile at Chelsie as if it were a flashlight. She smiled back weakly. His voice echoed out over the crowd, magnified by the microphone clipped to his shirt. "I'm so proud to be here today at" — he paused dramatically, as if for effect — "International High!" Only Chelsie and Lara could see Marie backstage, holding up cue cards with the name of the school on it. *He doesn't even know what school this is!* Lara realized with a jolt.

"But none of this would have been possible," Troy continued when the cheering finally died down, "without a letter written by a very special girl. And that girl is International High's very own Chelsie Peterson!"

Lara saw Chelsie's name written in block capitals on Marie's cue card. Chelsie saw the cue card, too, and Lara bit her lip. He hadn't known Chelsie's name, either.

"Come on out here, Chelsie," Troy roared. Chelsie stumbled out on the platform. The crowd went absolutely wild. They were chanting, "Chelsie, Chelsie!"

"Well, Chelsie, I think you've got something for me, don't you?" Troy flashed his famous smile.

Chelsie smiled back weakly, holding up the giant gold key. She'd memorized a whole little speech for this moment. "On behalf of all the students of International High, I offer you this key to —"

But apparently that was enough. Troy took the key neatly from her hand and held it high above the crowd. Now they were yelling, "Troy, Troy."

"And I have something for you, Chelsie." From a hidden place on the podium, Troy pulled a single perfect red rose. "The perfect flower for the perfect fan." He handed Chelsie the rose. The crowd went crazy again. Girls all across the audience were practically swooning. Even Principal Simmons was beaming.

Lara watched from behind the canvas screen, just a few feet away. She was the only one who knew the pain Chelsie had to be feeling. This was awful!

"Now," Troy said from the podium, "all you reporters have to go on home. I have to go be a principal!" He took Chelsie by the shoulder and swept her offstage in a giant wave of applause.

The second they were out of camera range, he dropped Chelsie like a hot potato. "Marie! Where's my bottled water?"

He pointed at Principal Simmons and Assistant Principal Merlin. "Are you in charge of meals around here? I need a fresh organic salad. Radic- chio and endive only, do you hear? Iceberg lettuce makes me break out in a rash." He waved his hands at them. "Get going!"

Marie pointedly said to Troy, "This is Principal Simmons and Assistant Principal Merlin."

"Oh, I thought they were the caterers," Troy said. "Sorry." He walked away.

The whole school was buzzing with excitement. All the girls gathered around Chelsie. Nichelle shrieked, "That was just the most romantic thing! Show us the rose."

Tori said, "Was it fun being up onstage with him?"

Chelsie held the rose out a little numbly. "It was fun being up onstage. But Troy wasn't like I thought he would be. Not at all."

"So he was better?" Ana said. "Oh, boy, this is so cool."

"Let the girl talk," Nichelle said. "How else can we find out what Troy is really like?"

"If you really want to know, Troy was really a jerk!" Chelsie said loudly. "And after that whole performance, everyone in the whole school thinks he's just the greatest guy in the whole universe."

Picture Perfect?

"Are you sure he's a jerk?" Tori asked, shocked. "But he looks so great! I mean, maybe he's just jet-lagged or something."

Lara said, "Just because he looked good from down here in the audience doesn't mean anything."

"What did he say?" Barbie asked.

Chelsie told them about what a creep he'd been. "And that's not all. Did you hear how he was ordering around Principal Simmons and Mr. Merlin? And how he treats his assistant, too? He just uses people."

Tori said, "Well, we're not putting up with that! Nobody talks to our Chelsie like that and gets away with it." She wrinkled her brow in thought. "So what can we do to teach him a lesson?"

Chelsie pulled the scrunchy out of her hair in aggravation. "Nothing. The whole school would elect him to be king. Nobody will listen to us at all."

And it turned out just that way. All morning Chelsie and the other girls tried to tell people what the real Troy Marcus was like. And all morning the girls had to stand and watch as Troy charmed the whole school, from the teachers to the students. He even kissed the hand of Mrs. Morgenthau, the cafeteria lady.

Just before lunch, Chelsie admitted defeat.

"Everybody loves him," she wailed despairingly. "They just don't know what he's like."

"She does," Barbie said, pointing at Marie Chung, who was on her cell phone frantically trying to order an organic salad for Troy.

"Where's Wonder Boy supposed to eat lunch?" Tori asked Marie when she finally hung the phone up in disgust.

Marie laughed out loud and then covered her mouth. "Don't tell him I laughed, okay? He's eating all by himself in Principal Simmons's office."

"Ms. Chung?" Assistant Principal Merlin called. He was carrying a big paper bag. "I went down the street to the health food market and had them make an organic salad for Mr. Marcus. Endive and radicchio only."

"Mr. Merlin, you are a lifesaver!" Marie exclaimed.

"Can I take the salad in?" he asked. "Maybe I can get to talk to him a little."

"Go right ahead," Marie said.

Mr. Merlin pushed open the door and went in.

The girls went into the cafeteria and sat down, sunk in depression. Even Mr. Merlin liked Troy!

Picture Perfect?

Suddenly the PA system crackled into life. Everyone snapped to attention. Was Troy going to make a special announcement? It didn't sound like an announcement.

Crackle, crackle. "You call this a salad, Mr. Whatever-Your-Name-Is? Look at how wilted the endive is! Doesn't anything get done right in this stupid school?"

There was more static, then Mr. Merlin's voice said, "You know, Mr. Marcus, I don't like you talking about our school like that. Our students are the finest young people in the whole city, if you ask me!"

Out in the cafeteria, there was dead silence.

"Yeah, well, look around at this crummy little office," Troy's voice echoed through the wall speaker. "This whole 'Principal-for-a-Day' thing has been a total waste of time. No publicity value at all. Just like that homeless shelter she dragged me to last month."

In the cafeteria, an angry murmur ran through the crowd of students. "Who does he think he is, the dumb jerk?" a boy said.

Crackle, crackle. Mr. Merlin sounded shocked,

even through the static. "I — I don't think you're a very nice person, Mr. Marcus."

"I've got a major motion picture to shoot, okay?" Troy said. "I don't have time to be nice."

Lara whispered in Chelsie's ear, "I've got an idea. Come on!" The two girls snuck out of the cafeteria unnoticed. The rest of the school was riveted by what was coming from the PA system.

Tori looked around the cafeteria a minute later. "Hey, where did Chelsie and Lara go?" she said.

Suddenly, Chelsie's voice rang out over the speaker, British accent and all. "This is Chelsie Peterson." She was in the office!

"What are you doing?" Troy Marcus's voice said. "Shut that thing off."

"It's too late for that, Mr. Marcus. But it's not too late for me to tell you what I think about you. You insulted our whole school and everyone in it. I was the fool who invited you. Now I'm going to uninvite you! Give me back that key! And I'm giving the key to the man who defended our school's good name: Assistant Principal Merlin!"

The whole cafeteria applauded. Now they were chanting, "Merlin, Merlin!"

Picture Perfect?

In the office, Lara squeezed her friend's hand. "Oh, Chelsie," she said, "that was perfect."

The school was in an uproar. Mr. Merlin came out of the office holding the giant gold key, with Chelsie and Lara by his side. Students cheered him from all sides. Mr. Merlin blushed. "Thank you all!" he stammered. "I'm honored to be your 'Principal-for-a-Day'!"

Troy Marcus slunk out behind him. Principal Simmons spotted him. "Your welcome has expired, Mr. Marcus! Good-bye," she said decisively. The students applauded again.

"Fine!" Troy said. "See if your school ever gets a photo opportunity like this ever again. Come on, Marie, let's go to the limo."

"I don't think so, Mr. Marcus," said Marie. She threw her briefcase and her beeper on the floor at Troy's feet. "No salary in the world is worth trying to make you seem like a human being. I QUIT!"

Troy stormed out of the building to his limo, all by himself. Not even one student followed him.

Chelsie looked upset. "Oh, Marie, I'm sorry. I never meant for you to lose your job!"

"Chelsie, honey, this is the best I've felt in almost two years!" Marie laughed. "I'm going back to L.A. to write that screenplay I've been planning. I've just been waiting for the right moment to quit. And you girls sure gave me the right moment!"

Chapter 10

Life Goes On!

Lara stood in an exhibition gallery at the Metropolitan Museum of Art. She still couldn't believe that the judges had selected her as a finalist in the New Artists' Competition. But now the judges were circling the room, looking at each exhibit one final time. They had to pick a winner.

Mama grabbed her arm, "Oh, Lara. The lady judge, she smiled when she walked by!"

Papa clasped his hands together, as if in prayer. "*Liebchen*, do you think you might vin?"

Lara sighed. She had so hoped that Mama and Papa would have decided to move back in together by now. But Papa was still in faculty housing at NYU, and she and Mama lived at the loft. Lara went back and forth between them, living with Mama during the week and with Papa on weekends. It wasn't fun, but she was getting used to it. They were all going to family counseling, too, which Lara didn't like at all. Oh, well, as Grandmama said, if life were perfect, we wouldn't appreciate the good things enough.

And there were lots of good things. Mama and Papa weren't fighting all the time anymore. That was a big one. And all her friends were there for Lara anytime she freaked out. She didn't have to ask for their help with a note hidden under a tile. She just knew it was there, anytime she needed it. And last but certainly not least, Lara had her art.

Barbie said, "Come on, Lara. They're going to announce the winners!"

"We're all keeping our fingers crossed for you," said Mrs. Johnson, the director of Rainbow House. All the students who volunteered at Rainbow House were there, too, which made Lara feel really good. Chelsie, Ana, and Nichelle held up their hands to show Lara that all their fingers were crossed for good luck. Tori whispered to her, "I've crossed my toes, too. So you're sure to win!"

The judges awarded third place, which came with a $1,000 prize, to a sculptor who combined clay with a laser-light show.

Then second place, which came with a $2,500 prize, went to a painter who combined papier-mâché with a beehive filled with live bees.

Finally, first place. Lara held her breath. She had no chance, she knew that. She'd been lucky to make it to the finals at all! But she couldn't stop hoping.

"And first prize in the New Artists' Competition goes to — Lara Morelli-Strauss!"

Lara's knees were weak as she went up to the judges' table to accept her $5,000 prize. She borrowed the microphone.

"My goodness," she heard one of the judges say, "she's so young."

"Age doesn't make art," said one of the other judges.

Lara cleared her throat. "I-I wanted to thank everyone who helped me so much. Mama, Papa, all my friends. I was going to buy all of you beautiful presents with the prize money, if I was lucky enough to win." Lara's voice broke. "But I think I found something better. I am giving my prize money in all of your names to help the Rainbow House shelter."

Mrs. Johnson's mouth flew open in surprise as Lara handed her the $5,000 check.

"I think you'll find a good way to use this, no?" Lara smiled.

"Yes, a hundred different ways!" Mrs. Johnson said. "Are you sure?"

Lara looked around the room, at her family and all her friends. "Yes, I'm sure," she said. "I already have everything I need."

GENERATI✳N GIRL™
available from Gold Key® paperbacks:

TURN THE PAGE TO CATCH
THE LATEST BUZZ FROM
THE *GENERATION BEAT* NEWSPAPER

GENERATI✱N BEAT

ARTISTS' COMPETITION FEATURES I.H. STUDENT

Artists all over New York were asked to create a mixed-media work that combines two or more different materials for the Metropolitan Museum of Art New Artists' Competition.

Recently Lara Morelli-Strauss, a sophomore at International High, entered the contest. Ms. Morelli-Strauss is a young artist who has done wonderful work here at I.H., and her artwork is excellent. "I am so excited to be a part of this competition. The other artists are so talented. I am honored to be among them," said Morelli-Strauss.

The artists in this competition have created many amazing pieces, including an unusual laser light artwork. The winner of this competition, who will be chosen at the exhibit next week, will be awarded $5000. If you are interested in new art, be sure to check out this exhibit at the Metropolitan Museum of Art, on Fifth Avenue at 85th Street.

WRITING FOR THE ENTERTAINMENT SECTION

Entertainment articles should cover what is entertaining to your audience. Whether you are writing about movies, music, art, or the theater, you can write in a lighter tone than you would in a news article.

How to write an entertainment article:

• Think of a subject. Everyone in your math class might be talking about the newest action film, or your older sister plays the newest CD from her favorite band over and over. Or maybe you can't miss a single episode of that new TV show on Sunday nights. When you notice this sort of thing happening, it's time to start writing!

• Research your idea. Entertainment articles are about what's hot and exciting in the world of movies, art, television, or music. One place to research ideas for your article is the Internet. Many celebrities have their own websites. Production  companies promote new movies heavily on the Internet. Search engines are a great way to find everything you are looking for. When you find something interesting, print it out and save it. You can keep a folder of entertainment research. That way, you can use it when you are out of ideas.

• Write the article. As always, write clearly and simply. Include a description of exactly what kind of entertainment you are reviewing, and be sure to include the address of where it is taking place.

People may want to see the movie or play that you are describing, so you have to make sure they know where it is and when it is taking place.

Remember: **WRITING=HONESTY=TRUTH**

DON'T MISS **GENERATI✱N GIRL** #6:

Nichelle is having a blast modeling sun dresses in Central Park in the middle of winter. But she's also got other things on her mind. There are rumors that the construction site downtown was once a burial ground. And Nichelle will stop at nothing to find out the truth.